# CATCH ME IF I

# Fall

Claudia Recinos Seldeen

An imprint of Enslow Publishing

WEST **44** BOOKS™

**Please visit our website, www.west44books.com.**
**For a free color catalog of all our high-quality books,**
**call toll free 1-800-398-2504.**

**Cataloging-in-Publication Data**
Names: Recinos Seldeen, Claudia.
Title: Catch me if I fall / Claudia Recinos Seldeen.
Description: New York : West 44, 2023. | Series: West 44 YA verse
Identifiers: ISBN 9781978596351 (pbk.) | ISBN 9781978596344
(library bound) | ISBN 9781978596368 (ebook)
Subjects: LCSH: Children's poetry, American. | Children's poetry,
English. | English poetry.
Classification: LCC PS586.3 R435 2023 | DDC 811'.60809282--dc23

First Edition

Published in 2023 by
Enslow Publishing LLC
2544 Clinton Street
Buffalo, NY 10011

Editor: Caitie McAneney
Designer: Leslie Taylor

Photo Credits: Cover (sky) cobalt88/Shutterstock.com, (trapeze)
ANGHI/Shutterstock.com.

Printed in the United States of America

CPSIA compliance information: Batch #CW23W44: For further information contact
Enslow Publishing LLC at 1-800-398-2504.

For Brandon, who has always
been perfect just as he is.

# BALANCING ACT

*Hang*
*on*
*tight!*

When I'm on a trapeze,
I defy gravity.

I'm a leaf
caught in a summer storm.
Twisting.
Spinning.

But there's always that voice
in the back of my mind,
whispering:

*Hang*
*on*
*tight.*

*Don't*
*let*
*go.*

*Falling is not an option.*

# DANCE TRAPEZE

When I tell people
I'm a
trapeze artist,
their eyes
light up
like stars.

I know
they're thinking about
flying
        trapeze.
About acrobats
w h i z z i n g
through the air.

But
dance
        trapeze
is
different.

There's no
swinging.
No catching.
No letting go.

A
dance
        trapeze
doesn't
tick tock
back and forth.

A
dance
       trapeze
spins
in tight circles.

It twirls
and turns.

If you don't hold on,
it will
spin
you
right
off.

# NOODLE

After every trapeze class,
I lie on my bedroom floor
and let the bruises
bloom.

That's what
no one tells you
about trapeze.

The bar is made of metal.
The ropes can slip
and burn.

When my mom
calls me for dinner,
I trudge
down
the
stairs
on wobbly legs.

If AnnMarie were here,
she'd call me a
noodle.

She'd flop her arms
like boiled spaghetti
and make me
laugh.

She can
always
make
me
laugh.

But AnnMarie
isn't here.

My best friend
can't come over
on trapeze days.

# GETTING IT RIGHT

*Angela,*
my mother says.
*How was trapeze class?*

*Good,*
I answer.
*We learned a new drop.*

My mother lifts
her head.

*Did you get it
right?*
she asks.

I think of
the drop.
A roll up
into the ropes.
A quick
release.
A dizzying tumble.
Like a snowflake
fluttering
to the ground.
My heart
thundered
when I tried it.

My breath
gasped.
My stomach
dipped.

But that's not
what my mother
wants to hear.

So I tell her
what she's waiting for.

I tell her,
*Yes.*
*I got it right.*

She
smiles.
And something inside me
swings higher
than a trapeze
ever could.

# IMMIGRANT

My mother
is a doctor.

She works from
sunup
to
sundown.

Before that,
she was an intern.
She worked
through the night
and slept in her clothes.

Before that,
she was in medical school.
Swimming
in an ocean
of textbooks.

*Immigrants,*
she tells me,
*have to work*
*twice as hard*
*just to shine*
*half as bright.*

My grandmother
came to the
United States
from
Guatemala.

But my mother
was born in
New York City.

I was born in
New York City.

When I tell
my mother
we're not
immigrants,
she says,
*Your grandmother*
*was an*
*immigrant.*

*To some people,*
*that's enough*
*to make*
*you*
*an*
*immigrant,*
*too.*

# SWIMMING

The days
leading up to
winter break
used to feel like
getting ready to
l e a p
off a diving board.

But now I'm in
high school.

Now,
the weeks
before
winter break
are filled with
due dates
and
exams.

Now,
the days feel like
kicking
and
fighting
just to keep my head
above water.

# SUCCESSFUL

In English class,
we learn about
personal essays.

*A personal essay,*
Mr. Pope tells us,
*should be a window*
*into your life.*

He tells us
to write about a time
we were
successful.

I think of all my
trapeze competitions.
All my trophies.
All my medals.

I lean back in my chair
and smile.

I could write
this essay
with my eyes
closed.

# I HAVE TRAPEZE

AnnMarie
slides into place
beside me
at my locker.
Her brown eyes
glimmer
like tinsel.
Her ponytail
swings back and forth.
She smiles,
and dimples
appear on her cheeks.
Like fingerprints
on polished glass.

*Homework*
*at your house?*
she asks.

I look up
at my best friend.
The end of her ponytail
is dyed bright pink.
Like a sunset
over water.

I want to say
yes!

But …

*I*
*can't.*

*I*
*have*
*trapeze.*

# A STAR

*I'm free tomorrow,*
I offer.

AnnMarie nods.
But her attention is
somewhere
else.

Her attention is
with
Gavin.

Gavin Scott is a
senior.

A
varsity hockey player.

A
star.

His locker is
down
the
hall
from ours.

But it might
as well be
the
other
end
of the galaxy.

AnnMarie and I
watch him
run his fingers
through hair
the color of a
nighttime sky.

*I'll see you tomorrow,*
AnnMarie says.

Then she drifts
away from me.

She drifts
toward Gavin.

A comet
pulled
into his
orbit.

# MISTAKES

My mother
is asleep
when I go into her room.

She's still wearing
her glasses.
She's still wearing
her shoes.
Books and papers
spill
across her bed.

I take
my mother's
glasses off.

She mutters
and rolls over.
And I wonder if she's
dreaming.

My mother had me
when she was
16
years
old.

Her boyfriend's parents—
my grandparents—
said I was a
mistake.

That I would
ruin
their son's life.
But my mom's mother—
my grandma—
stepped in.

She told them
my mother wanted nothing from them.

She told them
she and my mother
would raise me
all on their own.

I wonder,
sometimes,
if my dad regrets
never knowing me.

I wonder if my mom
dreams of a life
where she didn't get pregnant
at 16.

A life without
night school.

A life
without
mistakes.

I put my mother's glasses
on the nightstand.
Next to the silver-framed picture
of my grandma.

I step back
and watch my mom
sleep.

Even now,
her mouth is
pressed
tight.

Like she's
holding
her breath.

Like she's
holding in
a secret.

Like she's
holding back
a smile.

# DANCING

Sometimes
when I can't sleep,
I close my eyes.
I pretend
I'm on a trapeze.

In my head,
I lift
myself up
into the ropes.

I twist
and
pose
around the bar.

In my head,
I don't make
any
mistakes.

Or
get tired.

There's no voice
at the back of my mind
telling me I might
fall.

I tie
myself up
in knots.

I dance
in the air.

And
I
am
perfect.

# A CHANGE OF PLANS

The next day,
AnnMarie
finds me
in the hall.

She grabs my arm
and pulls me close.
She bounces
on her toes beside me.

*I found out
that Gavin
takes boxing lessons
Wednesday nights.*

She smiles
a smile
full of stars.

*Guess where we're going!*
she says.

Her hands
sweep the air
the way birds
sweep the sky.

*We're going boxing!*

# IT'S NOT THAT (I ONCE SAW)

It's not that
Gavin
isn't a nice guy.

(I once saw him
help
a lost freshman.)

It's not that
I don't
like him.

(I've never said
a word
to him.)

What bothers me
is the way
AnnMarie's eyes
gloss over
when he's near.
The way she
forgets
herself.

(The way
she forgets
me.)

# STILL ON

AnnMarie
is waiting
at my locker
after school.

*Are you ready
for our first boxing class?*
she asks.

I take a deep breath
and blow it out.

I have
homework.

I have
midterms.

I have
so
much
to
do.

But AnnMarie
leans forward.
The pink ends
of her ponytail
flicker
like stoplights
in the space
between us.

*Angela,*
she says,
*I'd do it*
*for you.*

# FAMILY

The first time
I met AnnMarie,
we were in third grade.

We were learning about
genetics.
Eye color.
Hair color.

*You inherit your physical traits*
*from both*
*your mother*
*and*
*your father,*
the teacher said.

She gave us a worksheet
to fill out.

Two parents'
names.

Two parents'
traits.

Two parents
to make
one
me.

I looked at the worksheet
and thought of
my mom.

My grandma.
How
it was just
the three of us.
And tears
scratched my throat.

But,
then,
AnnMarie
leaned across the space
between our desks.

*I don't have
a mom,*
she whispered.
*What do I do?*

I shrugged.
*I don't have
a dad.*

AnnMarie
studied me.
Her brown eyes
as round as quarters.
Then,
two dimples
appeared on her cheeks.

*Let's share!*
she said with a grin.

The two of us
filled in our sheets
with borrowed answers.

And by the end of class,
I couldn't tell where
her family
ended
and mine
began.

# WALK AWAY

The sign on the door says:
Amateur Boxing Club.

But the building is
flat roofed
and small.
The door
is painted black.
The windows
are tinted dark.

I think of the studio
where I take
trapeze lessons.
Sky blue walls.
High ceilings.
Pink and yellow silks
hanging like streamers
in the light.

I groan and
start to
walk
away.

But
AnnMarie
grabs my hand.

*I'd do it*
*for you,*
she reminds me.

And I know
I can't turn back
now.

# BEST FRIENDS

Anyone
can be
a friend
when it's easy.

It's when things get hard
that
best friends
stick by you.

You'd do it
for me.

       I'd do it
       for you.

That's what
best friends do.

# AMATEUR BOXING CLUB

Punching bags
hang
in the dimly lit space.

They remind me of the apple trees
in my grandmother's backyard.
The way the ripe fruit used to
weigh down
the branches.

A pinprick of grief
stings my heart.

I take a deep breath
and smell
sweat.
Oiled leather.
Dust.

Everything here seems
heavy.

Everything here is
flat.

Everything here
is like
balloons
filled with sand.

# COACH

A woman
stands
at the front
of the room.
Muscles
curve her arms.
Like the ripple
of sand dunes.
Her eyes
are sharp.
Her teeth
are straight.
Her skin
is the color of the
*cortaditos*
my mom drinks
when she's tired.

She puts
her hands
on her hips.
She plants
her legs
wide.
Her eyes glitter
like sunlight on snow.

*Welcome to boxing!*
she booms.
*My name is
Eleanor.*

*But you can call me
Coach.*

# FEAR

Our boxing coach
smiles a lot.
Fierce smiles.
Like
a brushstroke
of color
in the dark and dingy
room.

*If this is your*
*first time here,*
she says,
*you're probably*
*scared.*

She curls her fingers
into a fist.
A flower
blooming
in reverse.

*Put your fear*
*right*
*here,*
she tells us.

Then she
p u n c h e s
the tight bud
of her fist
against a
punching bag.

And she makes
        that bag
            fly!

# PARTNER

Coach tells us
to break up
into pairs.

I start to
reach
for AnnMarie.

But Coach
shakes her head.

*Don't pick*
*someone*
*you came with,*
she says.
*Pair up with someone*
*you don't know.*

AnnMarie shrugs
an apology.
Then she
turns around.
She walks away.

She
heads
straight
for
Gavin.

*Do you have a*
*partner?*
a voice asks
behind me.

I pull my eyes
away
from AnnMarie.

*No,*
I say.
*I guess*
*I don't.*

# CHANCE

My partner's name is
Chance.

*(As in:*
*take a*
*chance,*
he says.
*Get it?)*

I press my lips together
to hold in a groan.

Chance studies me through eyes
the color of buckwheat.
His hair is arranged
in dark twists.
Like the first shoots of spring.

I want to tell him
I'm not here to make friends.

But his smile
is quick and bright.
Like darting fireflies.

So I grit
my teeth
and say nothing.

# BOXING

I didn't bring
any boxing gloves.
So,
Coach lets me borrow
an old pair
from the lost and found.

I pull them on.
I wiggle
my fingers.
Like I'm waving
goodbye.

Chance stands
on the other side
of a punching bag.

Every time
the bag moves,
I catch a glimpse of
him.
        A shoulder.
An elbow.
        A smile.

He reaches out
and steadies the bag
between his hands.

*Go ahead,*
*short stuff,*
he says.
*Give it a punch.*

I think of
all the things
I should be
doing.
          Studying.
Homework.
          Mr. Pope's essay.

I squeeze my eyes shut
and shake my head.

I shove all my thoughts
inside one curled fist.

And
then
I
hit.

# SORRY

The punching bag
sails
backwards.

And hits Chance
right
in
the
face.

*Are you okay?*
I cry.

Chance's eyes are
round
and
startled.

But when he looks
at me,
he's
smiling.

*Yeah,*
he says.
*I'm great.*

I shake my head
and try to tell him
I'm sorry.

I
made
a
mistake.

But Chance holds up
his hand.

*Don't,*
he says.
*Don't be sorry.*
*That*
*was*
*amazing!*

42

# THINGS UNSAID

*How was trapeze?*
my mother asks
when I walk in
the door.

I open my mouth
to remind her
I don't have trapeze
Wednesday nights.

But then
I think of
what she'd say
if I told her
about boxing.

> Did you pay attention?
> Did you work
> twice
> as
> hard?
> Did you shine?

I think of how it felt
to hit the punching bag.
Like a flock of birds
lifting off my chest.

I don't tell my mother
about boxing.

I decide
to keep it to myself
for a while.

# JUST IN TIME

I wake up
the next morning
and realize
      I forgot
        to do my homework!

I scramble to finish
Mr. Pope's essay.
      On the subway.
      On the way to school.

My margins
aren't formatted.
There's no time for
spell-check.
But I finish
      right before
      I get to my stop.

I submit my essay
just
in
the
nick
of
time.

# MAYBE

AnnMarie finds me
at my locker
between classes.

*Hey there, boxing champ!*
she says.

She laughs
and bumps my shoulder
with hers.

*We should go boxing*
*again,*
she tells me.
*Gavin says*
*practice*
*makes*
*perfect.*

I feel a fist
curl
inside my chest.

The voice
in the back of my mind
starts listing
all the things
I have
to do.

*I have trapeze*
*tonight,*
I tell AnnMarie.
*I have*
*regionals*
*coming up.*

*And I*
*absolutely*
*have to study.*

The end of
AnnMarie's ponytail
dances on her shoulder.

*What about Friday?*
she asks.

The fist tightens
around my chest.

But AnnMarie is looking at me
like she's not going to
breathe
until I give in.

*Maybe,*
I tell her.

*Maybe …*

47

# IT'S SOMETHING

When I was
six,
my mom signed me up for
ballet lessons.

I felt like a princess
in my pink leotard
and my satin shoes.

But when I turned
seven,
my mom started
medical school.

Money
got
tight.
And I had to quit
ballet.

My grandma
stepped in.

She made some
phone calls.

She found
a circus camp
for low-income kids.

Kids whose moms
didn't have enough money
for ballet school.

Kids whose moms
were struggling
to make ends meet.

Kids like me.

*It's not ballet,*
Grandma told me,
*but*
*it's something.*

So,
I stopped crying
over tutus
and pink tights.

Thanks to
Grandma,
I fell in love
with trapeze.

# TRAPEZE CLASS

I squeeze my fingers
around the trapeze bar
and close my eyes.

Yesterday,
when I curled my hand
into a fist,
the whole world
went
quiet.

But,
today,
the voice
in the back of my mind
reminds me
to point my toes.
To keep my back straight.
It reminds me
that regionals
are right around the corner.
It reminds me
to lift my chin
and smile.

# SAY YES

I get AnnMarie's text
on the train ride
home.

*Boxing tomorrow?*
*(Say yes!)*


I look
out the window
and see my own
reflection
in the glass.

I look a lot like
my mother.
Dark hair.
Tired eyes.
Lips pressed tight.
Like I'm holding in
a secret.
Like I'm holding back
a smile.

I think of all my fears.
          Failing.
          Falling.
          Making a mistake.

I think of what it felt like
to put all those fears
in one curled fist.

And hit.
      And hit.
            And hit …

I thumb my phone
back to life
and look at AnnMarie's message.

I hold my breath
and type back,
*Okay.*

# MORE

The day
before winter break,
Mr. Pope
hands back
our personal essays.

*These are good,*
he tells us.
*But I want you to*
*dig*
*deeper.*

*What does it mean*
*to be*
*successful?*

He tells us
to rewrite
our essays.
He tells us
to hand them back in
after the break.

I raise my hand.

There must be
some kind of
mistake.
I'm not used to having papers
handed back
without a
perfect
score.

Mr. Pope sighs
and shakes his head.

*You can put your hand down,*
*Angela,*
he says.

*Everyone*
*is redoing the assignment.*

*I want you to*
*scratch beneath*
*the surface.*

*I want you to*
*get personal.*

*I want you to*
*tell*
*me*
*more.*

# BOXING GLOVES

On the way
to the boxing gym,
AnnMarie hands me
a brown shopping bag.

*What's this?*
I ask her.

She smiles
a smile
full of secrets.

*Open it,*
she says.

I open the bag
and find
a bright pink pair of
boxing gloves
inside.

*They're for you,*
she tells me.
*An early Christmas present.*

I take the gloves
carefully
out of the bag.

They feel strange
in my hands.
Hard,
like armor.

But also
delicate.
Precious.
Mine …

AnnMarie
bumps my shoulder
with hers.

She unzips her backpack
and shows me another pair of
boxing gloves
tucked inside.

Bright pink,
just like mine.

A matching
set.

Two
of a kind.

# WELCOME BACK

Coach grins at us
when we walk in the door.

*Welcome back,*
she says.

Then she claps her hands
twice.

*Hurry up!*
she shouts.
*Put your*
*things*
*down!*

*Find*
*your*
*place!*

# TAKING CHANCES

Chance's smile is
a pop of light.
Quick
and
bright.

*I'm ready for you*
*this time,*
he says.
*I'm not taking any*
*chances.*

*Get it?*
he asks.
*Chances?*

I groan
and shake my head.

But his smile
only grows wider.

*Let's go,*
*short stuff,*
he says.

He holds the punching bag
steady
between us.

*Let's go,*
he says.
*Give it*
*all*
*you've*
*got.*

# 60 SECONDS

We're supposed to
punch the bag
as many times
as we can
in one minute.

At first,
I count
each punch.

But
after 20 seconds
the voice
finds me.

The voice
that's always there
in the back of my mind.

The voice
that's always telling me
that I'm not trying hard enough.
That I have to
be better.
Do more.

The voice hits me
with its words.

But I
grit my teeth.

And I
hit
back.

# QUIET

After 60 seconds,
I fall on my back.
Sweaty and
out of breath.

I close
my eyes
and wait to hear
what the voice
has to say.

But everything
is quiet.

The voice
in the back of my mind
has fallen
silent.

# WINTER BREAK

Winter break is my favorite.
Hushed skies.
Frozen puddles.
Drifting snow.

When I was little,
my mom would drop me off
at Grandma's house.
Then she would head off
to medical school.
She was always
at medical school.

Grandma and I used to take
long walks
in the snow.

We would talk about
school.
Circus camp.
AnnMarie.

She would listen
while I talked.
Her breath
a white cloud.
Like frozen feathers.
Soft.
Safe.

Grandma died
when I was 12.
And my world
shrank down.
Like a soap bubble.
My world became
me and my mom.
My mom and me.

But Mom works
all the time.
So it's mostly
just
me.

I throw on my boots
and go outside.

I lie on my back
on the frozen ground.

I watch
the snow
float
softly
from a sky
the color of silver.

I pretend
Grandma is lying
right beside me.
Her breath
making white clouds
in the cold air.

If my mom saw me,
she'd say,
*Think how much training time*
*you'll miss*
*if you catch a cold.*

But my mom
isn't home.

And my puffy jacket
feels like a lifeboat.
Rocking me
on a gentle current.
Carrying me
into an open sea.

# HOT CHOCOLATE

AnnMarie comes over
in the afternoon
and we make
big, steaming mugs
of hot chocolate.

We sit on the floor
and watch the snow
through my bedroom window.

*There's another boxing class*
*on Monday,*
I say.

She wraps both hands
around her mug.

*Don't you have*
*trapeze*
*on Monday?*
she asks.

I do.
I have trapeze classes
three days
a week.

So what's the harm
if I miss one?

I lift my
hot chocolate
to my face.
The steam feels
warm
on my cheeks.
Soft,
like feathers.

*What if Gavin
isn't there?*
AnnMarie asks.

I stifle the urge
to roll my eyes.

*What if he's there,*
I say,
*and you miss him
because you didn't show up?*

I can tell
by the way AnnMarie grabs
the end of her ponytail
that I've made
a good point.

*Boxing on Monday?*
I ask.

*Yeah,* she sighs.
*Okay.*

# WORK

Winter break
used to mean
sledding.
Sleeping late.
Slumber parties.

But now we're in
high school.

Now,
our teachers assign enough work
to last the entire week.

AnnMarie has to write
a research paper
on World War II.

I have to rewrite
my personal essay
for Mr. Pope.

So, the two of us turn away
from the window.

We sit in the middle
of the bedroom floor.

We pull out our backpacks
and get to work.

# WINNING

I frown down
at my personal essay.

Four pages
about dance trapeze.
About winning.
About being successful.

Mr. Pope's comments
are in purple ink
along the top.

*This is good,*
the purple ink tells me.
*But there's no
emotional connection.*

I shake my head.
My frown deepens.

I wonder
how Mr. Pope can say
there's no emotion
in my writing?

Winning
is an emotion
I've known half my life.

# MERRY CHRISTMAS

When I was a kid,
my mom and I
used to celebrate *Noche Buena*.
Christmas Eve.

Grandma used to come over and
the three of us
sat around the tree.
We ate
my grandma's
homemade tamales.
We opened gifts.
I fell asleep
on the couch
nestled between
Grandma
and
my mom.

But,
now,
it's just
the two of us.
Just me
and my mom.

Now,
we celebrate on
Christmas morning.
We exchange our gifts
over breakfast.

And then my mom
gives me
a quick hug.

We say,
*Merry Christmas!*

And then my mom
goes
to
work.

# MONDAY'S CLASS

Gavin
is there
at Monday's boxing class.

But Chance
isn't.

I open my mouth
to make a joke
about
missed chances.

But then
I snap my mouth closed
again.

The only person
who'd get the joke
isn't there to hear it.

# FORGET

Gavin waves
at AnnMarie
from across the room.

He smiles
and runs his fingers
through hair
as glossy as
crow's feathers.

AnnMarie
bounces lightly
on the tips of her toes.
She turns her head
and grins at me.
And then she
glides
toward him.
Like a kite
being led
by a string.

I pull on
my boxing gloves.
Like I'm pulling on
a bulletproof vest.

I curl my hands into
fists.

And I forget
about AnnMarie.

About Gavin.

I even
forget
about Chance
for a while.

# A REAL FIGHT

After class,
Coach walks up to me.

My fists
are numb
My legs are shaking.
My face is covered
in sweat.

But when Coach smiles,
I can't help
smiling
back.

# BOXING

*I was around your age,*
Coach says,
*when I started*
*boxing.*

She lifts her hand
and makes
a fist.

*I was under a lot*
*of pressure*
*back then,*
she says.

She opens her hand
like she's letting
something
go.

*Boxing*
*made all those pressures*
*go away.*

She drops her hand
to her side.

She tips her head
and studies me.
*How would you like*
*to train for*
*a boxing match?*
she asks.

*How would you like to learn*
*how*
*to*
*really*
*hit?*

# FITNESS EXPO

There's a Fitness Expo
in two weeks.

All of the fitness centers
in the area
will be there.

Our boxing gym
is putting up a ring
right
in
the
middle
of it all.

*It's just for fun,*
Coach says.
*But if you're interested,*
*there's a spot*
*open*
*for a beginner.*

# HARD WORK

*We'll have to get you in*
*fighting shape,*
Coach says.
*Even beginners*
*can pack*
*a punch.*

I flex my hands
inside my gloves.

My muscles
are already strong
from trapeze.

But I've only ever hit
a punching bag.

I don't know
how to fight.

*It'll be hard work,*
Coach warns.

*Do you think*
*you can do it?*

I think of trapeze.
I think of school.
I think of my mother.

*I can do it,*
I tell Coach.

I've been working hard
all my life.

# I'M OKAY

My mom
is in her room
when I get home.

*Angela,*
she calls.
*How was trapeze?*

I drop my bag
on the kitchen table.
I drag myself
across the hall.
I flop
onto the bed
beside her.

When I was little,
I used to bring my
picture books
into my mother's room.
I'd sit
on the bed and
flip
through
the pages.
The same way
my mother
flipped
though her textbooks.

I used to tell her
I was going to be a doctor
just like her.

I was going to be
just
like
her.

*Angela,*
my mother says.
*Is everything okay?*

I'm tired.
I'm worried about school.
About trapeze.
About boxing.
But I close my eyes.
I take a deep breath.

*I'm okay,*
I tell her.

And when I open my eyes,
my mother is smiling.

# IN CASE OF EMERGENCY

Last summer
I worked as a counselor
at my aerial gym's camp.

I saved
all the money
I earned.
I put it
away.
I kept it
safe.

I promised to use it
only for
emergencies.

But boxing classes
are expensive.

My allowance
won't cover
three boxing classes
a week.

So I dip
into my savings.
I pay for more
boxing classes.
I don't even think about it twice.

# BAM!

There's something so satisfying
about the sound of a punch
connecting.

It's a thud.
Like a heartbeat.
Like my heart saying,
*I'm alive!*

Coach teaches me how to use
my whole body
to hit.

She shows me how to jab.
How to hook.

One, two.
One, two.

BAM!
BAM!

The room is filled
with the sounds
my fists make.

The sounds I make
using my own
strength.

# HIGH FIVE

Chance is back
at boxing
on Wednesday night.

At first,
I worry that Coach
won't let us pair up.
That she'll make me
pair up
with someone new.

But,
to my surprise,
Coach claps her hands twice
and nods.

*Take her in the ring,*
she tells Chance.

*Teach her
to spar.*

Chance looks at me,
one eyebrow
raised.

*You're learning
to fight?*
he asks.

I feel my face flush
with warmth.
But I force myself
to nod.

Chance holds one hand up
for a high five.

*I knew
you were cool,*
he tells me.

Then he flashes
one of his lightning smiles.
And I smile back.

# THE RING

Stepping into the ring feels
like crossing over
into another world.

I duck under the ropes
and step onto
padded canvas.

My steps feel different
inside the ring.
Softer.
Sturdier.

My body feels different
inside the ring.
My heart beats faster.
My breathing slows.

I
feel
different
inside the ring.

Like someone
I don't know yet.

Like someone
I'm excited
to meet.

# FOOTWORK

Chance teaches me
how to duck.
How to bob.
How to weave.

He tells me,
*The best way to make sure*
*you don't get hit*
*is to*
*get out*
*of the way.*

He has me hold my hands up
in front of my face
like a shield.

And then he takes
a couple of
slow swings.

I duck under them.
I bob out of reach.
I weave back and forth.

*You're light*
*on your feet,*
Chance says.
*That's good.*

His swings come at me.
Faster and faster.

I slide one way.
And then another.
We move around the ring.
Eyes locked.
Arms swinging.

The whole world
falls away.

And it almost feels
like the two of us
are dancing.

# CATCH MY BREATH

I sit next to Chance
at the edge
of the boxing ring.

*You did good,*
he tells me.

*You did well,*
I correct.

He rolls his eyes
and turns away.

But not before
I catch the quick pop
of a smile.

# LOVE

Chance tells me
he's been boxing
since he was
eight
years
old.

I tell him
I've been training
on a trapeze
since I was seven.

*Wow,*
he says,
*You must really love it,*
*to have stuck with it*
*for so long.*

I think
of the way
my heart trips
when I'm in the air.
The way
it feels
to hold on tight.

I think
of the way
my mom looks
when she watches me
perform.

She hardly ever
smiles
since Grandma died.

But when she's watching me
on a trapeze,
her eyes
light up.

Her face
relaxes.

And she
smiles.

I must love trapeze,
I think to myself.

I must.
I must.

# STARS

*Do you think Gavin*
*will ever ask me out?*
AnnMarie sighs.

We're sitting
at the kitchen table.
Textbooks
like tarot cards
spread between us.

I put my essay aside
and frown.

I want to tell AnnMarie
not to get her
hopes up.

Gavin is a star.
And stars
don't usually see much
beyond their own light.

But AnnMarie
is smiling.
Her eyes are shining
like full moons.

So I bite my lip
and nod.

# RACE

My mom calls me
downstairs
for dinner.

If AnnMarie
were still here,
she'd try to race me.

But it's Sunday.
And AnnMarie
went home
hours ago.

I run
down the stairs
anyway.

Even though I'm tired.
Even though I'm sore.
Even though
there's no one there
to see me
win.

# DINNER

When I was a kid
my grandmother
used to come over
every weekend.

She'd play card games
with me
while my mom
was studying.
Old Maid.
Go Fish.
Memory.

She would make dinner.
Pupusas.
Empanadas.
Rellenitos.

The smell of
onions and garlic,
sugar and cinnamon,
would hang
like paper lanterns
all over the house.

Once in a while
when my mom cooks dinner,
I catch the scent
of frying peppers.
Refried beans.
Fresh tomatoes.
And it's like Grandma is with us
again.

Just for
a little
while.

# GIFT

After dinner,
I wait for my mom
to ask
about trapeze.

But,
to my surprise,
my mom
doesn't ask.

Instead,
she scoots her chair back.
She pulls a box
from under the table
and sets it
in front of me.

*I know*
*Christmas is over,*
she says.
*But I saw this*
*online the other day*
*and I couldn't resist.*

I lift the lid
carefully.

I push aside
tissue paper.

Bright blue fabric
shimmers
like dewdrops
in the sun.
I stare,
wide-eyed,
at the prettiest
trapeze costume
I've ever seen.
Sometimes it's still
hard to remember
that we're not poor
like we once were.

*It's for
the trapeze regional competition
next week,*
my mother says.

*You'll want to look
your best
when
you
win.*

# PERFECT

*Do you like it?*
my mother asks.

It takes
a minute
for me to find my voice.

*I love it!*
I tell her at last.
*It's*
*perfect!*

My mother
smiles at me,
eyes shining.

*Just like you,*
she says.

*Just*
*like*
*you.*

# FLAWLESS

I've won first place
at trapeze regionals
every year
since I was 10.

(Every year,
except the year
Grandma died.)

Each year,
my trapeze teacher
comes up with a routine.

I learn it.

And then I
practice.
And practice.

Over
and
over.

Until it's
flawless.

Until
I'm
flawless.

# STRETCH

My body feels like
one
long
knotted
rope
when I wake up.

So I sit
on the hardwood floor
and
s t r e t c h.

I have
trapeze
tonight.

I have
boxing
the day
after.

It's a lot.

But I can't miss
either one.

# PRACTICE

When I was in seventh grade,
I twisted my shoulder.

I had to stay off the trapeze
for
        six
                weeks!

I lost
so
much
practice
time.

That was the year
Grandma died.

That was the year
I didn't win
first place
at regionals.

That was the year
I learned
that
practice
makes
perfect.

# PUSH

When I try to pull myself
onto the trapeze,
my legs feel heavy.
My back is stiff.
My shoulder complains.

I've been doing
too much.
I haven't been resting
enough.

I take
a deep breath.

I push
past the pain.

I work
twice as hard
as I usually do.

I tell myself
I can rest
later.

When regionals
are over.

When I've won.

# WHAT'S GOING ON?

My trapeze teacher
pulls me aside
after class.

*The competition is in*
*three*
*days,*
she says.

*Your routine was*
*messy.*

*Your transitions were*
*sloppy.*

*What's*
*going*
*on?*

My stomach
twists itself
into knots.

*I'm just a little tired,*
I say.

My trapeze teacher
lets out a quiet sigh.

*Go home,*
she tells me.

*Get*
*some rest.*

*And then come back*
*tomorrow*
*and practice!*

# I DON'T TELL

I don't tell
my trapeze teacher
I have boxing
tomorrow.

I don't tell
my trapeze teacher
about boxing
at all.

# WHAT WOULD YOU DO?

AnnMarie
can't come over
on trapeze days.

But that night,
I close the door
to my room.
I sit on the floor.
I call her up.

*I can't miss*
*boxing,*
I tell her.
*But I can't miss*
*trapeze,*
*either.*

I slide down
onto my back
and stare up at the ceiling.

*I could catch the train*
*right after boxing,*
I say.

*I could make it*
*to the aerial studio*
*just in time.*

I grip the phone
in my hand
and close my eyes.

*What would you do,*
I ask,
*if you were me?*

AnnMarie
laughs.

*If I were you,*
she says,
*I'd be too*
*tired*
*to move.*

# READY

Coach
makes us do
warm-up drills
before we can start boxing.

Jumping Jacks.
Squats.
Lunges.

I rush through them.
As impatient
as a kid
racing through shallow water
to get to the
deep end.

*Ten more push-ups!*
Coach shouts.

I groan
and drop to the floor.

The voice
in the back of my mind
creeps forward.
It tells me
I'm moving too slow.
It tells me
this is taking too long.
It tells me
there's no way
I'll make it
to trapeze practice
on time.

# FOCUS

Chance
leads the way
into the ring.

*Teach her to keep*
*her guard*
*up,*
Coach calls.

So Chance
has me hold my hands up
while we dance around the ring.

*Always*
*keep your eyes*
*on your opponent,*
he says.

I wonder
what time it is.
I wonder
if I can stay
15 more minutes
and still make it
to trapeze.

One gloved hand
sweeps out
and taps me on the cheek.

*You let your guard*
*down,*
Chance tells me.
*Keep your hands up.*

And just like that,
the voice
in the back of my mind
starts to scream.

# ALARM

I take a deep breath
and try to focus.

But my attention drifts
to the clock
on the wall.

Chance taps me
again.

*You're not concentrating,*
he says.

The voice
in the back of my mind
R O A R S,
  *Try harder!*
  *Do better!*

Chance straightens.
*Your opponent*
*is trying to*
*hit you,*
he says.

*Don't give them*
*the*
*chance.*

*Get it?*
he asks.
*Don't give them*
*the*
*chance …*

The voice
in the back of my mind
becomes a fire alarm.
      *You're going to*
      *fail!*

I press my gloves
to my head
and close my eyes.

*I don't have time*
*for this,*
I growl.
*I don't have time*
*for stupid jokes!*

# GUARD

I hold my boxing gloves
up to my mouth.
Like I could snatch the words
out of the air
and take them back.

I try
to apologize.

But Chance
shakes his head.

His smile
is slow and heavy.
His smile
has lost its light.

*I guess that's what happens,*
he says,
*when you let your guard
down.*

# GUESS WHAT

Chance climbs out of the ring
without looking back.

After a while,
I do the same.

I pack up
my gloves.

I head
for the door.

But AnnMarie
catches me
before I can slip outside.

*Guess what!*
she whispers.
*I've made a decision!*

I give her
a thumbs-up.

But AnnMarie
snatches my hand
out of the air.

She pulls me closer.
*I'm going to be brave,*
she says.

*I'm going to ask
Gavin out!*

# NEVER MIND

AnnMarie waits
for me to say something.

She waits
and she waits.

After a while,
her smile wavers.

And then it
disappears.

*AnnMarie,*
I say at last.
*Gavin is like …*
*a celebrity.*
*He's*
*a star.*

AnnMarie blinks.
She takes a step
back.

*And what am I?*
she asks.

*You're amazing!*
I say.
*But Gavin …*

AnnMarie
drops my hand.

*Never mind,*
she says.

She points
at the clock on the wall.
Like she's throwing something
across the room.

*You'd better go,*
she says.
*You don't want
to be late.*

And then she turns
and walks away.

# SHOULD

I know
I should go after
AnnMarie.

But she streaks
away from me.

She heads
straight
for
Gavin.

Gavin's brows come together
over eyes the color of
rain clouds.
He leans down and says something
I don't hear.

Twin dimples appear
on AnnMarie's cheeks.
Like handprints
on wet sand.

And I realize she's smiling.
She's laughing!

She doesn't
need me
after all.

# TALK

I take only
three steps
out the door
before Coach catches up with me.

Her usual
fierce smile
is gone.
Wiped away.

In its place
is a frown.
Like
the first dark cloud
in an otherwise sunny sky.

*I was watching you*
*in the ring,*
she says.
*Is there anything*
*you want to talk about?*

The wind
whips around me.
Sharp
and
cold.
But my face
flushes hot.

*I had a hard time*
*concentrating*
*today,*
*I tell her.*
*I've got*
*a lot*
*going on.*

Coach studies me
a minute.
Then she nods.

*My first boxing match,*
*she tells me,*
*I was under*
*so much pressure*
*to win.*

*I know how you feel,*
*she says.*

*You're not*
*alone.*

*I'm here*
*if you ever want to talk.*

# SO CAN I

On the subway,
I think of all the trophies and medals
hanging on the boxing gym's walls.
The ones that catch the light
like Christmas ornaments.
The ones that flash at the edge of my vision
every time
I climb into the ring.

Coach and I
aren't that
different.

We're both
fighters.

We're both
winners.

Coach understands
what I'm going through.

If Coach
could handle the pressure
when she was my age,
then
so
can
I.

# UNDER THE WIRE

I make it to trapeze class
just as my phone
tells me it's six o'clock.

I make it to trapeze class
just
under
the
wire.

# ROUTINE

I run through my trapeze routine
three times.
But it still doesn't feel right.

The music
moves faster
than I do.

I can't catch my breath
between poses.

I can't remember
what comes next.

In the end,
I have to cut
most of the harder moves.

To make up for it,
I add something new.

I add
the drop
I learned two weeks ago.

A roll up
into the ropes.
A quick
release.

I can
do this.
I
have
to
do
this.

Falling
is not
an option.

# THE DAY BEFORE

The day
before regionals,
I wake up
to find my mom
sitting on the edge
of my bed.

*I have to go to work,*
she says.
*But I wanted to make sure*
*you take it easy*
*today.*

My arms wobble
when I sit up.

But I can't help
a smile.

The day
before regionals
is the only day
my mom tells me
to take it
easy.
To slow
down.
To rest.

*Will you be back*
*for New Year's Eve dinner?*
I ask.

My mom nods.
*I'll be back,*
she says.
*But you should go to bed*
*early.*

*You need to rest*
*today.*

*So you can win*
*tomorrow.*

# NEW YEAR'S EVE

The last day
of the year
is quiet.

Usually,
I spend the day
before regionals
watching old movies
with AnnMarie.

But this year
is different.

AnnMarie
doesn't call me.

       I don't call
       her.

This year
I stay home
by myself.

# IN MY HEAD

That night,
I close my eyes.
And
I pretend
I'm at regionals.

In my head,
I
lift
myself up
onto the trapeze.

I
see the audience
below me.
Smiling.
Clapping.

In my head,
I dance
in the air.

And
I
don't feel tired.

I am
graceful.

I am
flawless.

I am
perfect.

# ON THE TRAIN

My mother
sits next to me
on the train
on the way
to regionals.

New Year's Day
is one of the few days
she takes off of work
every year.

One of the few times
I see her like this:

Dark hair,
loose
around her shoulders.
Eyes shining.
Smile
after
smile
flashing like neon lights
across her face.

# REGIONALS

I walk into
an auditorium
overflowing
with chattering voices.

A girl
in a pink leotard
races past me.

A woman
holding a clipboard
calls out names.

My heart
starts drumming
as I look around
the buzzing room.

The slim
triangle shape
of a dance trapeze
catches my eye.

I take a deep breath
and blow it out.

*I can do this,*
I tell myself.

I give my mother
a quick hug.

And then I start
working my way
through the crowd.

# BACKSTAGE

The other contestants
chat and hug.
They squeal over each other's
costumes.
They fuss with each other's
hair.

I know
almost everyone.

I've been competing with them
since I was a kid.

But I don't smile
or giggle
or hug.

I stand off to one side,
like my mother taught me.

This isn't
a reunion.

This is
a competition.

And I'm here
to win.

# THIS IS IT

The announcer
calls my name.
And the voice
in the back of my mind
sighs.

*This is it,*
it tells me.

*Don't*
*mess*
*it*
*up.*

# POSE

My body feels
tense.
Like a string
pulled as tight
as it will go.

But
I stand
in front of
the trapeze
and smile.

The music is
louder
than I expected.
I can feel
the bass
inside my chest
like a second heart.

I grab the bar.
My hands
are sweating.
But I pull myself
up.
I slide one leg
into the ropes.
I pose.
The knot
in my stomach
loosens
a tiny bit
when I hear
the audience clapping.

I keep going.
Keeping time
with the music.

I thread an arm
around the bar.
I catch my ankle.
I arch my back.

The audience claps again.
And I begin to
relax.

But I hold
the second pose
a little longer
than I was supposed to.

The music
moves on
without me.

The voice
in the back of my mind
starts to chorus an alarm.

I rush through
the next few poses
to catch up.
My breathing feels loud
in my ears.

My body is struggling
to keep up.

I put all my effort
into holding my last pose.
And then all I have left
is the drop.

I roll up
into the ropes.

I count to
three.

A quick
release.

A
dizzying
tumble.

And then
something goes
horribly
wrong.

# FALLING

I
fall.

Like an autumn leaf
fluttering
to the ground.

Except it's
not
pretty.

It's
not
graceful.

I slip out
of the trapeze.
And hit the safety mat
with a sickening
thud.

And then
there is nothing
but silence.

# I DON'T WIN

I don't win
the trapeze regional competition
that year.

I don't
even
get an
honorable
mention.

# SIGH

When we get home,
my mom
sighs.

*Do you want*
*to talk about it?*
she asks.

I shake my head.
I don't want to talk.
What is there to say?

My mom
sighs again.
A loud rush of air.
Like it's the only way
to get all the
disappointment
out of her body.

*There's always*
*next year,*
she says.

I turn around.
And walk
very
slowly
up the stairs.

The sound of my mother's
sigh
follows me
all the way
up.

I imagine
I can hear
her sigh
even when I clap my hands
over my ears
and cry.

# THE VOICE IN THE BACK OF MY MIND

*You*
*messed*
*up.*

*Everyone*
*saw you*
*fall.*

*You didn't work*
*hard enough.*

*You failed.*

*You failed.*

*You failed …*

# THE FIRST DAY BACK

The first day back to school
after winter break
used to be filled with
excited sharing.
New backpacks.
Smiling friends.

But now,
we're in
high school.

Now,
the first day back
is filled with
sleepy-eyed yawns.
Misplaced assignments.
Teachers reminding you
that winter break is over
and it's time
to get back
to work.

# NOTHING TO TURN IN

Mr. Pope collects
our personal essays.

But I
didn't finish
rewriting
mine.

I have
nothing
to turn in.

# MR. POPE

After class,
Mr. Pope pulls me aside.

*It's not like you
to miss an assignment,*
he says.

I nod
and look
down
at my hands.

*Is there anything
you'd like to talk about?*
he asks.

I shake
my head.
I know
if I try to talk
I'll start crying.
And if I start crying
I don't know
if I can stop.

Mr. Pope
is quiet
a while.

*You know,*
he says at last,
*everyone gets*
*overwhelmed*
*from time to time.*

*Take*
*a couple of days.*

*Work*
*on your essay.*

*Hand it in by*
*the end*
*of the week.*

# THAT CAN WAIT

AnnMarie
finds me
at my locker
after school.

She doesn't
smile.

She looks at me
like I'm
made of
glass.
Like she's searching
for a crack.

*I heard
about regionals,*
she says.

I groan
and cover my face
with my hands.

*From my mom?*
I ask.

AnnMarie nods.
*She called my dad.*

I swing my locker
closed.
*I hope you don't have
any plans,*
AnnMarie says.

I peek at her
out of the corner of my eye.

*I thought
you were
mad at me,*
I say.

*I am,*
AnnMarie sighs.
*But that can wait.*

She flips her ponytail
over one shoulder
and gives me
a half-hearted grin.

*Right now,
we're
going
boxing.*

# GOOD FOR YOU

I don't want to go
boxing.

I don't want to go
anywhere.

I just want to go
back home
and crawl under the covers.

But AnnMarie's mouth
tightens.

*I've seen the way*
*you look*
*when you're hitting*
*a punching bag,*
she says.

*It's the*
*same way*
*you used to look*
*when you jumped on*
*a trapeze.*

She grabs my arm
and gives me a
sharp tug.

*Come on,*
she says.
*We're going.*

*This will be*
*good*
*for*
*you.*

# WHAT IF?

When we reach
the boxing gym,
the voice
in the back of my mind
starts to mutter.

*You failed at trapeze,*
it reminds me.
*What if you fail
at boxing,
too?*

I try to turn around.
But AnnMarie
grabs my hand.

She pulls
the door open.

She walks
inside.

And I have
no choice
but to follow.

# PUNCHING BAG

I pull on
my boxing gloves
slowly.
Like I'm not sure
I should be doing it.
Like I could stop
at any time.

I stand
in front
of the punching bag.

I curl my hands
into fists.

I hit.
Softly,
at first.
Then harder.

I hit.
And I hit.
And I hit.

Until my arms
are shaking.

Until I can barely
catch my breath.

# EVERYTHING

Coach walks up to me
after class.

*AnnMarie told me what happened*
*at trapeze regionals,*
she says.
*Do you want to talk about it?*

I take
a deep breath.

I don't want
to talk.

I just want to
run away.

But I'm so tired
from hitting the punching bag.
I don't think
I can move.

I open my mouth
to tell Coach
I messed up.

But, instead,
I tell her
everything.

About trapeze.
About regionals.

About my mother.
I tell her about the voice
in the back of my mind.

How it's always telling me
I'm going to fail.

How I'm afraid
it's right.

# WINNING AND FAILING

Coach nods.
Like this is a story she's heard before.
Like she's about to tell me how it ends.

*When I was your age,*
she says,
*I was under so much pressure.*
 *To fight.*
 *To get ahead.*
 *To win.*

I lift my head and look at all the
trophies and medals on the wall.

*But you did win,*
I tell her.
*You didn't fail.*

Coach laughs
softly.

*Oh, Angela,*
she says.

*I fail*
*all*
*the*
*time.*

# COACH'S STORY

*When I first started boxing,*
*I lost*
*half a dozen*
*fights*
*in*
*a*
*row.*

*And then*
*I got better.*

*But,*
*even now,*
*I win some*
*and*
*I lose some.*

*That's life.*
*That's being human.*

*You can't*
*be perfect.*

*And if*
*you try to*
*be perfect?*

*You'll*
*fail.*

# TICKETS

Coach tells me
to talk to Chance
before I leave.

I make a face.
Like she just suggested
eating raw eggs.

But she tells me
Chance is in charge
of selling tickets for the Fitness Expo.

I look down at my feet
and sigh.

I don't think
I can talk
to Chance
after the way
I acted.

And I
know
he doesn't want
to talk to me.

# A SKY FULL OF STARS

I look up and see AnnMarie
standing across the room
with Gavin.

Something twists
like a trapeze rope
in my stomach.

I watch Gavin run his fingers
through his dark hair.

And then I see him
smile.

I see his cheeks
turn pink.

I see him look at AnnMarie.
Not the same way
she looks at him.
Not like she's
a star.

But like she's
a whole sky
full
of
them.

# LOSING

It's not that I don't want
AnnMarie to be happy.

(She's been my best friend
since we were eight.)

It's not that
I don't want her
to go out with Gavin.

(She can date
whoever she wants.)

It's the way it suddenly
feels like
there's no room
for anyone else.
Not when
the two of them
look at each other
like that.

It's the way
she looks
like she's won
something.

(The way I feel
like I've lost.)

# WINNING

But maybe
that's okay.

Maybe losing
is okay
once in a while.

Especially
if it means
my best friend
in the whole world
wins.

# GETTING UP

Chance slides up beside me
while I'm watching AnnMarie.

*If you're going to buy*
*Expo tickets,*
he says,
*now's your chance.*

I wait for him to ask me
if I get it.

(*Now's your*
*chance ...?*)

But he only stares
at me.
His face as blank
as a winter sky.

I think of Coach
losing her first
six fights.

I picture her
getting back up.
Six times
in a row.

I take a deep breath.
*I'll take four tickets,*
I say.

The voice
in the back of my mind
whispers,
*You could fall.*
*You could fail.*

But
I've already fallen.
I've already failed.

And
I
survived.

# SECOND CHANCE

Chance hands me
four tickets.

But I give him
one of the tickets
back.

His face crinkles
in confusion.

*This one is for you,*
I tell him.

Heat floods my cheeks.
Like I'm tipping
my face
over a steaming mug
of hot chocolate.

*I know I was
a jerk,*
I say.
*I was hoping
you'd give me
a second chance.*

I straighten my
shoulders.

*Get it?*
I force myself to say.
*A second
chance …?*

Chance stares at me
for a minute.
And then
he rolls his eyes.

*Short stuff,*
he says.
*That was terrible.*

He hands my ticket
back to me.
And my heart
tumbles.

But then his face
lights up.
Like a gasp of sunlight
through clouds.

*I don't need a ticket,*
he says.
*I get in for free.*

*I wouldn't*
*miss your first fight.*

*Not a*
*chance.*

# A VERY LATE
# CHRISTMAS PRESENT

AnnMarie
walks with me
to the train station.

But she doesn't say
a word.
Neither of us do.

I know
she's still a little angry.

I know
she's right to be.

But before
we reach the subway entrance,
I grab her arm.

I take a breath
like I'm about to let go
of a trapeze bar.

And then I pull out
two tickets
to the Fitness Expo.

*What's this?*
AnnMarie asks.
*A very late
Christmas present,*
I say.

*Also,*
*an apology.*

AnnMarie raises
one eyebrow.
She takes
the tickets from me
and looks them over.

*For you and me?*
she asks.

I shake my head.

*For you*
*and Gavin,*
I tell her.
*For when*
*you ask him out.*

*For your*
*first date.*

# YOU'LL SURVIVE

AnnMarie
laughs.

But then her laugh
melts into
a frown.

*What if I ask Gavin out,*
*and he says no?*

*What if*
*he would've said*
*yes,*
I say,
*and you never find out*
*because you didn't*
*ask?*

I can tell
by the way she reaches
for her ponytail
that I've made
a good point.

I think of the way
Gavin looked at her.
The way he
saw
her.

*He won't say no,*
*I tell her.*
*But if he does,*
*you'll survive.*

*And I'll be right here*
*with you.*

# QUIET

My mother
and I
are like ships
gliding
past one another.

We don't talk
about trapeze.

We don't talk
about anything.

We move
around one another.

We are
as quiet
as sailboats.

# THIS ISN'T ABOUT TRAPEZE

After dinner,
I reach into my pocket
and pull out
a folded envelope.
I slide it
across the table toward
my mother.

My mother's shoulders
drop.
Her face
softens.
Her eyes sink down
to the envelope
on the table.

She opens it
and pulls out
a single ticket
to the Fitness Expo.

After
what feels like
an hour,
she looks up at me.

*What is this?*
she asks.

*It's for you,*
I tell her.
*So you can come watch me.*

Her brow
creases and folds.

*Watch you do what?*
she asks.

I force myself
to look my mother
in the eye.

I take a deep breath
and I say,
*Boxing!*

The word comes out
in one big rush.

Like a
shout.

Or a laugh.

Or a breath of fresh air.

# I DON'T KNOW

*Boxing*
*makes me happy,*
I explain.

*The way trapeze*
*used to make me happy.*

My mother's eyebrows
come together
in a knot.

*Are you saying*
*you want to quit*
*trapeze?*
she asks.

She spits
the word
"quit"
out like a lemon seed.

*No,*
I say.

Then,
*Maybe.*

And finally,
*I don't know.*

# DIFFERENT

*I love trapeze,*
I explain.
*But I don't like the constant pressure
to win.*

My mother sets the ticket down
on the table.

She folds her hands together
like she's praying.

She looks at the ticket.
And then she looks at me.

*I'm glad you found something new,*
she says.

*But how is this
any different
from trapeze?*

*You'll still have to
practice.*

*You'll still have to
compete.*

*You'll still have to
win.*

# WORDS

That night
I sit on my bedroom floor.

I open my laptop
and try to work on Mr. Pope's essay.

But all I can think about
is my mother's words.

All I can think about is
boxing.
Trapeze.
What it feels like
to practice.
Until I'm flawless.
Until I win.

Mr. Pope's question
runs through my mind.

*What does it mean
to be
successful?*

I look around my room.
The trophies on my bookshelves.
The medals on my walls.

I think of the year
I hurt my shoulder.
The year we lost
Grandma.
The year
it felt like
there would never be
light
or laughter
in the world
again.

I didn't win
trapeze regionals
that year.

But I didn't
give up.
I knew
Grandma
would have wanted me to
keep
trying.

So I took care of
my injured shoulder.
I bandaged
my bruised heart.
I tried again
the next year.

And
I
won.

But,
maybe,
it's not the first-place medal
that made me
successful.

Maybe,
what made me
successful
was climbing back
on the trapeze.

Maybe,
being successful
means trying.
Again and again.
Picking yourself up
after you fall.

# MR. POPE'S ESSAY

By the time
my phone says
it's bedtime,
I've finished
writing.

I sit
back.

I stretch
my arms
over my head.

I submit
Mr. Pope's essay.

And then
I close
my laptop.

I lay back
and close
my eyes.

I don't even notice
when I fall
asleep.

# SEE ME

My mom
has to work
the day of the Fitness Expo.

So I ride
the train
by myself.

I don't ask if she'll
get off work
in time
to see me fight.

I don't want to know
what it would feel like
to hear her
say no.

# ISLAND

The Fitness Expo
is a beehive hum
of activity.

Banners and posters
line the walls.

Tables
crowd the floor.

And in the center of it all
stands the boxing ring.
An island of royal blue.

I lift my bag higher
on my shoulder.

I tilt my chin
up.

And I head
straight for
the center of the room.

# LET'S DO THIS

Chance finds me standing
at the edge of the ring.

*You're up first, short stuff,*
he says.
*Are you ready?*

I hold my breath.

I don't want
to lose.

I don't want
to fail.

Chance gives me
the lightning pop
of his smile.

*Let's do this,*
he says.

*Go
get
'em.*

# LAST MINUTE

I'm about to climb into the ring
when I hear someone
call my name.

I turn around
and see my mom
pushing through the crowd
toward me.

She waves
at me.

She smiles.

And my heart swings
wide open.

# I WOULD DO IT
# ALL OVER AGAIN

*I wasn't sure*
*you'd make it,*
I tell my mom.

*I know,*
my mother says.
*I wasn't sure*
*I would,*
*either.*

Her smile dims.
Then disappears.

*Angela,*
she says,
*I know I've been pushing you*
*to work hard, lately.*
*It's what my mom*
*used to do to me.*
*And I hated it.*

*But there's a reason*
*she pushed.*

*There's a reason*
*I push.*

*I don't want you*
*to make the same mistakes*
*I made*
*when I was your age.*
Something threatens
to knot itself
in my heart.

I've never heard
my mom
talk about her
mistakes.

I've never heard
my mom
call
me
a
mistake.

My mom
sags
like a loose sail.

She reaches out
and pulls me
into a hug.

*When I was your age,*
she whispers,
*I made*
*a*
*mistake.*

*But*
*I would do it*
*all over again.*
*Because you're*
*the*
*best*
*thing*
*that ever happened*
*to me.*

*You're my Angela.*
she says.

*You're*
*my daughter.*

*You'll always be*
*perfect*
*in my eyes.*

186

# PERFECT

My mom's words
echo
in my head.

I've spent so much time
trying to be
perfect.

And all this time,
my mother already thought
I was.

Mistakes can change
your plans.
Mistakes can change
your life.
But mistakes don't have to mean
the end of the world.

I look up at my mom
and smile.

She smiles
back.

And something inside me
shines brighter
than any trophy
ever could.

# AUDIENCE

I stand
inside the ring.
I take
a deep breath.
I count
to 10.

Out of the corner
of my eye,
I can see
the audience.

Coach
watches me.
Her smile as fierce
as a smoking volcano.

Chance
claps and grins.
*Short stuff,*
he calls.
*You can do this!*

AnnMarie
sits next to Gavin.
The pink ends of her ponytail
flicker and dance.
She leaps to her feet,
pulling Gavin up with her.

My mom
stands at the edge of it all.
Eyes shining.

Brow furrowed.
Lips pressed together.
Like she's holding in
her worries.
Like she's holding in
all her fears.

When I was little,
I used to want to be
just
like
my
mom.

But, now, I know
I can't be afraid
to fail.
To fall.

I have to be
myself.

I have to
let all those fears
go.

# WHAT MATTERS

I face my opponent
inside the ring.

She's taller than I am.
Dark curls peek out
from under her headgear.
Muscles stand out
on her shoulders and arms.
Like the swell of waves
on a stormy sea.

I hold my hands up
the way Chance taught me.

*Hang*
*on*
*tight!*
the voice
in the back of my mind
tells me.

*Don't*
*let*
*go.*

*Falling is not an option.*

I take
a deep breath.
And I tell the voice
to be
quiet.

I replace the voice
with the memory of my Grandma.
The way she looked
walking beside me
in the snow.

Falling
is an option.

Falling
is a very real possibility.

It's not the fall
that matters.

What matters
is what I do
after.

What matters
is that I pick myself
back
up.

I picture Grandma
looking down at me.
Her breath a white halo
around her proud face.

I look at my mom
standing at the edge of the ring.
She catches my eye
and nods.
She cups her hands
around her mouth.

*I love you always,*
she shouts.
*Win or lose.*

I put all my fears
in the palms of my hands.

I make
two fists
around them.

My opponent
looks at me
and snarls.

I dance toward her.
I wait for an opening.

And then
I
hit.

# WANT TO KEEP READING?

If you liked this book, check out another
book from West 44 Books:

## *NO PLACE FOR FAIRY TALES*
### BY EDD TELLO

ISBN: 9781978596320

# Once Upon a Time

there was a girl named Azul
who lived in a poor,
colorful *vecindad*
in Monterrey, Mexico.

*Even though Mom calls it*
*mini-apartments.*

This is not
how fairy tales are supposed to start,
but I will be clear:

        this is not a fairy tale.

In our vecindad,
fairy-tale dreams

        *\* shiny tiaras and long gowns \**

usually don't come true.
Not for people like us.

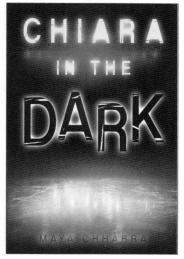

## CHECK OUT MORE BOOKS AT:
www.west44books.com

An imprint of Enslow Publishing

WEST **44** BOOKS™

# ABOUT THE AUTHOR

Claudia is a Miami native who currently resides in Western New York. She is the author of the young adult novel *To Be Maya*. Her poetry has appeared in *The Amphibian Literary Journal* and *MONO*. Claudia is a first-generation Guatemalan American. When not writing, she is either playing video games with her husband and son, or flying through the air on a trapeze. Find out more at www.recinosseldeen.com.